Noises at Night

Written by Tom Ottway

Illustrated by Juanbjuan Oliver

Collins

Who's in this story?

Listen and say

Mum

Jodie

Download the audio at www.collins.co.uk/839772

2 Kane and Jodie are sleeping in their new beds in their new house.

5

Jodie says, "Kane, listen ... can you hear that?"

Kane says, "What?"

Jodie says, "That noise ..."

Kane says, "I can't hear it.
Go to sleep!"

7

Jodie says, "Kane! What *is* that noise?"

Kane says, "*SSSSHHH!* I'm sleeping!"

Jodie says, "No, listen!"

Kane says, "It's the tree!
On the window."

Go to sleep, Jodie!

Kane says, "Jodie! There isn't a noise in our cupboard!"

Jodie says, "Yes, there is. MUM! DAD!"

SCRAAATCHH

Daddy says, "Now go to sleep please, Jodie!"

Look in *the cupboard*, Daddy! Please!

13

The cat runs away.

They look … and look …
Then they find the cat in the kitchen.
It's small and young. It's a kitten.

Jodie says, "It has a name!"

Mummy says, "Its name is Tinki. And there's a phone number!"

In the morning, Mummy phones the number. A woman answers the phone.

She says, "Do you have my kitten, Tinki? Thank you! I'm very happy!"

The woman comes to the house.

Thank you for finding my kitten!

Daddy says, "Let's get a kitten for our family!"

Picture dictionary

Listen and repeat

cupboard

kitten

scream

window

1 Look and order the story

2 Listen and say

Collins

Published by Collins
An imprint of HarperCollins*Publishers*
Westerhill Road
Bishopbriggs
Glasgow
G64 2QT

HarperCollins*Publishers*
1st Floor, Watermarque Building
Ringsend Road
Dublin 4
Ireland

William Collins' dream of knowledge for all began with the publication of his first book in 1819.

A self-educated mill worker, he not only enriched millions of lives, but also founded a flourishing publishing house. Today, staying true to this spirit, Collins books are packed with inspiration, innovation and practical expertise. They place you at the centre of a world of possibility and give you exactly what you need to explore it.

10 9 8 7 6 5 4 3 2

ISBN 978-0-00-839772-2

Collins® and COBUILD® are registered trademarks of HarperCollins*Publishers* Limited

www.collins.co.uk/elt

British Library Cataloguing in Publication Data

A catalogue record for this publication is available from the British Library.

Author: Tom Ottway
Illustrator: Juanbjuan Oliver (Beehive)
Series editor: Rebecca Adlard
Commissioning editor: Fiona Undrill
Publishing manager: Lisa Todd
Product managers: Jennifer Hall and Caroline Green
In-house editor: Alma Puts Keren
Project manager: Emily Hooton
Editor: Tessie Papadopoulou-Dalton
Proofreaders: Natalie Murray and Michael Lamb
Cover designer: Kevin Robbins
Typesetter: 2Hoots Publishing Services Ltd
Audio produced by id audio, London
Reading guide author: Emma Wilkinson
Production controller: Rachel Weaver
Printed and bound by: GPS Group, Slovenia

MIX
Paper from
responsible sources
FSC **FSC™ C007454**
www.fsc.org

This book is produced from independently certified FSC™ paper to ensure responsible forest management.

For more information visit: **www.harpercollins.co.uk/green**

Download the audio for this book and a reading guide for parents and teachers at www.collins.co.uk/839772